Tales from Brierybank

All My Own Stories

Easy to Read

Selected by Meg Daniels

GEDDES & GROSSET

Published by Geddes & Grosset, an imprint of
Children's Leisure Products Limited

© 1997 Children's Leisure Products Limited,
David Dale House, New Lanark ML11 9DJ, Scotland

First published 1997
Reprinted 1999

ISBN 1 85534 171 9

Printed and bound in India

Contents

King Brownie and the Grocer

The Grocer and his Ways

In a pretty little village, in the time of the fairies, there lived a greedy grocer. He was so selfish and mean that he could only be called a miser. He lived only to make and save his money.

This grocer was the richest man in the village. Yet he was so greedy, that he never had even a penny to spare for poorer people.

If a poor beggar came to his door, to beg for a crust or for some scraps of meat, he would storm at him

angrily. Then he would drive him from his shop with a thick stick. He kept this stick especially for beggars.

It was no use anyone trying to get a bite or a sip from the stores of the greedy grocer. He never gave a thing away and he did not even feed himself properly! He thought it was waste of food to eat a good meal.

He used to save all the rinds of bacon, crumbs of cheese, and dusty odds and ends from his shop. These, with a few crusts and old bones, were enough for him.

He ate just one meal a day—his supper—and often he was content with food that would have made a mouse turn up its nose! Oh! he was a real miser, there was no doubt about that.

He put all his money into old socks, which he kept hidden halfway up the chimney. "My precious fortune will be quite safe there," he said to himself, "for I never light a fire."

He often cheated people who came to buy from him, particularly if they were old or had poor sight. As they could not see the scales, they did not know what he was doing with the food he was selling them.

Sometimes he put tiny stones and grit in his raisins and currants, sand in the sugar and bits of dead leaves in the tea!

He never had a kind word or a smile for anybody. It was a wonder that anyone would go to his shop at all. But his was the only shop for many miles around, so the village people just had to go there, and be cheated.

Mind you, he only cheated the old people, and poor widows and little children. You see, they were too weak or too young to stand up for their rights.

Some of the village women would not go to do their daily shopping until their husbands came home from work. Then they would go together to the shop, and the miser would not cheat them as he was afraid of their husbands.

What the Children Did

At last the village children made up their minds to go and see the Brownie King and ask him what to do. You see, there was no other shop where they could buy biscuits and sweets, when they had a little money to spend.

This was very sad for them. They did not dare to go near the greedy grocer now. They had teased him so many times that he would not serve them at all.

The village children were full of mischief. As they came back from school, they used to dance into the doorway of the shop, and shout at him.

Then the miser would rush out in a rage with a piece of rope in his hand, and chase them down the lane. The naughty children would run away laughing, for they knew very well that the old grocer would never catch them. They were much too quick and he was much too stiff to run far.

But they had now got rather tired of this little

game. They felt that it would be much nicer if the miser would give them sweets sometimes. They wished he would even let them buy things from him when they had a few pennies to spend.

So they took their troubles to the Brownie King. He sat on a fine big scarlet toadstool in the middle of the woods. Other tiny brownies were perched on plain mushrooms round about. Little King Brownie put on his magic thinking cap at once and said, with a merry laugh;

"Ha, ha, ha! Just you leave it all to me, my dears! I know the very thing to do! Tonight I'll play a trick on him that he will never forget! Ho! ho! ho!

"Don't worry your little heads any more. You'll see, I'll make the greedy grocer a kind grocer yet! Ha, ha, ha! Ho, ho, ho! He, he, he!"

Oh, how all the little brownies laughed! They tumbled off their mushrooms and rolled over and

over on the mossy ground! And the village children all laughed too.

Then they thanked the Brownie King for promising to help and off they trotted home to bed. They felt well pleased with their visit. They were quite sure their little brownie friend would do as he had said.

Night in the Grocer's Shop

That night the greedy grocer sat in his shop all alone. He always did, because he never asked a neighbour to come in for a chat or a cup of tea.

There he sat, without a fire or a light to cheer him. It was a cold night, and he was stiff in every bone. But he thought it was a "shocking waste" to burn even a small candle. So he took his supper in the dark, and sat on a hard stool. This was the only seat he had in his shop—it was just a miser's way!

As he sat there munching a hard crust, he chuckled to think how well he had cheated poor old Mrs Brown that morning, when she had come in to buy a few things.

"Ha, ha, ha! What a clever person I am!" he said aloud. "Silly old thing! She doesn't know her sugar is mostly sand and that there is chalk in her flour! What fun it is to get good money for the bad stuff I sell! Ha, ha!"

When he remembered how he had driven a beggar boy from his door and hit him over the head with a biscuit tin, he chuckled more and more!

Then, suddenly, he heard a strange noise in the shop—a sound of scuttling feet that soon stopped his chuckling and made his hair stand on end. Next

a clattering of pots and pans turned him quite white. Then he heard the sound of hundreds of matches being struck and then there was a blaze of light!

A Strange Sight

Such a strange sight now met the staring eyes of the greedy grocer. What do you think had happened?

All the groceries had come to life and were trotting round the shop on funny little legs! They all had arms and heads as well, and laughed and chatted with each other, very glad to be all together at such a jolly party.

And oh! It was a funny sight to see one pot of jam walking about arm in arm with a fat Cheshire cheese, while another danced with a ham! And jars of pickles, tinned fruits and bottles of tomato sauce were to be seen, chatting with the cakes of soap. How pretty the soaps looked in their dresses of pink and green!

Lords and ladies dressed in wigs and satins, had stepped out of the pictures on the lids of the biscuit boxes and were dancing a jig in the middle of the floor.

Now they were bowing before starting a new dance, while the others looked on. Round the wall, fat sacks of flour sat like old ladies, watching the dancers and talking with their friends, the tall sides of bacon.

The wax candles stood on the shelves in rows. Each had on its cap of flame. The matches too had come out of their boxes and had struck their heads alight, their tiny flames adding to the brightness.

This last sight was more than the greedy grocer could stand. The shock of these strange happenings had at first taken his breath away. But as soon as he had got it back, he cried out in a rage:

"What wicked waste is this I see going on before my very eyes? How dare you use up my precious

goods? Oh, oh, you'll set the shop on fire for sure! Just put out your flames at once, I say!"

"Indeed we shall do nothing of the kind!" said the candles, flickering happily. "We like having bright lights on our heads, and we don't mean to put them out for a long time yet!"

With these words, the wax candles and the matches burned all the more brightly until the shop looked more like a giant birthday cake for somebody with a great many birthdays than a grocer's shop.

The Grocer is Punished

Now the other groceries began to crowd round the miser. They all began to talk at once, then shout at him until he was nearly deaf with the din!

"Of all the mean and selfish people," they cried, "you are the very worst!" The greedy grocer drew back, trembling, into the far corner of the room.

"There is no doubt about that," they said. "You should be ashamed of yourself. We will not belong to such a horrid cheat any longer! So we have made up our minds to teach you a lesson.

"But we will give you the choice, either you turn over a new leaf or suffer what you deserve. You must give us your promise at once never to cheat your customers again, but always give good food and full weight—a thing you have never done before! And you must promise also to be polite and kind to everyone, both young and old.

"So now, old skinflint, promise you will behave better after this. If not, you must prepare for war with your groceries. So, beware!"

The greedy grocer had listened to this long

scolding too much amazed to speak. But now he cried out in a great rage: "How dare you speak to me? I promise nothing. I care for nothing but money! A miser I have always been and a miser I'll remain!"

On hearing this, all the groceries rose up in the air, with loud yells. Then they flung themselves on the miser. And he fell helpless to the floor.

The poor greedy grocer! It was like being in a snowball fight. Only it was much worse; for instead of soft snowballs, he was hit by pieces of ham, large sides of bacon, enormous round cheeses, sacks of flour, cakes of soap, boxes of biscuits and pots of jam and pickle.

Then the candles too came rushing down to join in the fun. "Hip, hip, hooray!" they cried, and they were soon joined by the bold little matches.

Lastly, the socks filled with money, which had been so carefully hidden, came clattering down the black chimney hole. Down they fell like a shower of silver upon the miser's back!

This was really more than the greedy grocer could bear. Struggling with his foes, he called aloud for mercy. "Stop! Stop! Stop! My dear groceries, stop at once, I pray you!" he cried.

"I will now promise to be a better grocer after this, if you will only let me live! I promise I shan't be a miser any more, I will be kind to everyone. Please stop! I will be good for the rest of my days!"

No sooner had he said this than the lights faded. The shop grew dark again, the hubbub was still and all became as usual.

Next Morning

The greedy grocer now knew that the war was over, and he was free once more. But all that night he never stirred. He lay still upon the floor where he had fallen when the angry groceries had set upon him.

And as he lay there, a great change came over him. It seemed to him that soft fairy voices were whispering kind thoughts from all around him. Soon these kind thoughts began to fill his heart. They filled it so full there was no room left for selfish thoughts at all.

With these kind thoughts in his heart, the grocer began to feel happy for the first time in his life. He made up his mind to be a greedy miser no longer and at last he fell asleep.

When he woke up at dawn next morning, he felt so light-hearted that he began to whistle and sing as merrily as a lark!

He would not keep on the old clothes he had thought good enough to wear for so many years. He took out instead, from the bottom of an oak chest, a suit of plum-coloured cloth. In this he dressed himself with great care. He then washed his face and brushed his hair. When he had finished he looked so neat and smart that no one would have believed him to be the shabby, greedy grocer.

Next he had a good look round his shop and was

glad to find that the groceries were safe and sound. They looked as if they had never stirred from their places.

He then set to work to clean out the shop and light a fire. Before lighting the fire he took down the socks filled with silver coins. They had been hidden long enough in the black chimney hole.

He put them instead in a handy drawer and also took care to fill his pockets with handfuls of silver. He meant to make good use of his money now. Instead of keeping it for himself, he would give most of it away to the poor and hungry.

As soon as the fire had burnt up, he cooked himself a good breakfast. It surprised him to find how much he enjoyed it. "How foolish I have been," he said, "to eat only old crusts and bacon rinds all this time! I could have had nice tasty food every day."

Making Friends

Presently the village children came hurrying past on their way to school. The grocer ran out of his shop and called them in. He wanted to give them some sweets and biscuits.

The little ones were at first afraid and surprised at the grocer's bright clothes and tidy appearance. But when they saw that he was pleased to see them, they went in, and soon they were full of smiles, as they thanked the grocer kindly for his sweets and biscuits.

When the children went on their way to school that morning, they were singing and skipping along with happiness.

Just then a beggar boy came along. It was the same boy who had been so badly treated by the greedy grocer only the day before. So he crept round the back of the shop, hoping to find a crust or an old bone that had been flung out for the birds.

But the grocer saw him, and to the boy's surprise,

he called him into the shop, and set a good meal before him. While the hungry boy ate, the grocer hunted about among his stores. At last he found what he wanted—a new suit of clothes for his young guest.

He gave the boy the suit, then asked him to live with him and help him in the shop. With a glad smile, the boy thanked the grocer, tied on an apron, and began to work at once.

A little later, several of the village women came into the shop to buy food. They were anxious in case they should find the grocer in a bad temper.

They had quite a shock when they saw him in his smart plum-coloured clothes, and heard his cheery greeting. However, they were delighted to find that the money they had brought went twice as far as usual, because the grocer served them generous measures.

Mrs Brown

Later that day, poor old Mrs Brown came in. She said bravely that she could not eat the bad bacon the grocer had sold her the day before.

To her delight, she was now given a large piece of fresh bacon and a fine basketful of other groceries. And not a penny was she charged for them! Besides this, the grocer asked her to sit by his fire and drink a cup of nice hot tea. So when Mrs Brown went home, she certainly had a fine tale to tell her neighbours.

"Whatever can have happened to change him so?" the villagers asked. "Till yesterday he was greedy and mean. Far from giving us presents, he would not even give us fresh food when we paid him good money for it.

"You say he is wearing plum-coloured clothes, and that he even asked you to have a cup of tea with him! Well, now! Wonders will never cease! Something very strange must have happened."

"Perhaps the fairies have paid him a visit," said Mrs Brown. "I used to be told the fairies can work wonders by just whispering in a person's ear! But, however it has happened, the greedy grocer is greedy no longer, but a nice kind man.

"What is more, he asked me to have tea with him again, the next time I visit his shop. And I shall certainly go soon! "Why, dear me! Here is some money in my pocket! It was not there when I left home. That kind grocer must have slipped it in when I wasn't looking! I shall buy a new scarf with it tomorrow."

A New Name

After this, everybody in the village hurried to call in at the shop of the greedy grocer. They were afraid they might be too late. Perhaps they might find his pleasant manners had changed back again to grumpy ones.

But they need not have feared anything of the kind. The greedy grocer never went back to his old ways. He was now much too busy trying to make other people happy to have time to think about himself at all.

To rich and poor alike, the grocer was now as polite as could be. He was never known to take a meal by himself if he could get some poorer person to share it with him.

He never cheated anyone or gave poor measures again. And when his poorest customers came for a pound of anything, he always gave them two.

He even spent his money on feeding and clothing any hungry people he heard of. When beggars came to his door, he would give them a few coins, even before they began to plead!

As for the children, they grew so fond of the kind grocer that there were always some of them to be found in his shop laughing and chatting with him, and telling him stories about school. They never left without wishing him a friendly goodbye.

And since the miser's heart had changed so much, they thought it was a shame to call him the "Greedy Grocer" any longer. Surely he had earned a better name! So they began to call him the "Generous Grocer" instead. And that is how he was known until the end of his days.

Fun with the Brownies

The children were so pleased with what the Brownie King had done for them, they felt it would be polite to pay him a second visit, just to thank him.

So one evening when it was getting dark, just before bedtime, they all went to the woods.

Here they found the Brownie King, holding a grand party. All the little brownies were having a wonderful time!

The sun had gone behind the hills long ago and

darkness had almost set in. Yet here, at the Brownie Court, it was as light as day. The sparks from hundreds and hundreds of glow-worms shone like tiny bright stars on every side.

The Brownie King was sitting on his big scarlet toadstool watching a ring of fairies and brownies dancing to a lively tune. The children were delighted with the pretty scene before them. Some of them wanted to join in the fun, but others said:

"No, we must thank the Brownie King first. Besides, we have not been invited to the party!"

So all the children went up to the scarlet toadstool and bowed before the Brownie King. Then one of them said:

"We thank Your Majesty very much indeed, for changing the greedy grocer into a nice, kind man."

Now, the Brownie King was very pleased the children had not forgotten to thank him for his kindness. "Such polite children should have a treat before they go," he said to himself.

So he invited them all to join in the fun of the merry party. And what a jolly time they all had!

The girls danced in a ring with the fairies, and the boys played leapfrog with the brownies. After this, they all played hide-and-seek in and out among the flowers and bushes.

At last the moon came out and it was time to stop. So the little visitors said "Goodbye and thank you!" to the Brownie King. Then they hurried home, as quickly as they could.

After this, the village children always said the jolliest time they had ever spent was at the Brownies' Party. And they never forgot the night they went to thank the Brownie King, for changing the greedy old miser into a Generous Grocer.

The Cherry Cobbler

The Cherry Cobbler is a little gnome whose job it is to look after cherries. Sometimes he polishes them, sometimes he paints them, sometimes, if they have fallen, he puts a little cherry-glue on them and sticks them on the tree again. He knows a lot about cherries—almost as much as the Cherry Wizard— but the Cherry Wizard is always looking for new cherries while the Cherry Cobbler stays at home and can always be found if you want him.

The Cherry Cobbler used to live on Cherry Green, but one day he had to move to Cherry Common.

The Cherry Cobbler had gone on an errand when the Big-Blow Wind came tearing across the Green on his way to a tempest (which is a kind of wind-party). Just as he got to the Cherry Cobbler's little wooden house he gave a very big blow, and blew the little wooden house sideways.

"Dear me, I am sorry about that," said the Big-Blow Wind to himself, "for the Cherry Cobbler is such a useful little fellow. But, never mind, if I blow from the other side I can soon put the house right again."

And with that he swept round the Cherry Cobbler's little house and gave a big blow from the other side—*phew!*

Alas, that was too much for the little house and instead of righting itself, it fell down flat, rattle-bang-flop!

"Well, I *am* sorry about that!" cried the Big-Blow Wind. "But I can do nothing about it." And away he went.

So there lay the Cherry Cobbler's little house, as flat as if it had been made of cardboard instead of wood.

His little wooden stool lay with its legs in the air, his porridge pan had rolled under a bush and his cupboard with five shelves hung on the bough of a nearby tree.

The Cherry Cobbler was halfway home from his errand when he met the Bun Wife, who was driving her little brown-and-white pony to market to sell her big buns and her little buns. The Bun Wife wears a white sunbonnet, a white dress and a white apron, and looks as if she was covered in her own baking flour.

When she saw the Cherry Cobbler she cried, "Alas, my little Cherry Cobbler, I have a piece of bad news for you. The Big-Blow Wind has been over Cherry Green and he has blown so hard that your little wooden house has fallen to the ground!"

When the Cherry Cobbler heard this dreadful news he was very sad and two large tears, rolled down his cheeks. "Oh no," he cried, "how am I to sit on my little wooden-stool and rest, and how am I to make my porridge, and how am I to tidy my cupboard?"

But the Bun Wife said, "Calm down, Cherry Cobbler, I do have a piece of good news for you, so things might be worse. Let me tell you this; the Treasure Witch is leaving her little house on Cherry-Common. She was putting her treasures in the carrier's cart as I passed by and so far no one has heard of this. So if you hurry, you may be able to get the Treasure Witch's house. And on my way back from market I will fetch your wooden-stool and the other things that were in your little wooden house. I looked at them, and they don't seem to be damaged or dented."

When the Cherry Cobbler heard this he felt a little better and dried his tears. Then he thanked the Bun Wife and flew away.

The Cherry Cobbler wears a red smock, the colour of a ripe cherry, and cream socks, and he has a pair of tiny green wings which are rather like cherry leaves. On these wings he flew to Cherry Common.

There was the Treasure Witch looking most upset. "I cannot find Treasure Number Six," she said, "and I do not remember what Treasure it was, but I *do* remember packing it."

"Perhaps it is in the cart," said the Cherry Cobbler.

But the Treasure Witch said rather crossly, "No, it is not in the cart. I have looked there and so has the carrier."

And the carrier said in a firm way, "It is *not* in the cart."

So they all three searched everywhere else for Treasure Number Six, but none of them found it.

"Oh well," said the Treasure Witch, "I must be getting on my way. Perhaps it was only a small Treasure that anyone who finds can keep."

"Dear kind Treasure Witch," cried the Cherry

Cobbler, "may I live in this little house, for my own house has been blown down by the Big-Blow Wind?"

"Can you pay a rent of one small jar of cherry jam a month?" the Treasure Witch asked.

"Yes, I can pay it," said the Cherry Cobbler.

"Then that is settled—you can have the house," said the Treasure Witch. And off she went in the carrier's cart, pleased to have rented her little house to someone so useful.

She was only just out of sight when who should come along but the Bun Wife, who had sold her big buns and her little buns very quickly and was now loaded with all the things that had been in the Cherry Cobbler's little wooden house.

"Ah, here you are!" she cried. "Tell me, my little Cherry Cobbler, have you seen the Treasure Witch, and are you going to live in this little house?"

"Yes, I am, at a rent of one small jar of cherry jam a month," said the Cherry Cobbler. "I'm so happy! And it is all your doing, Bun Wife."

"Oh, I don't know about that," said the Bun Wife. "She knows you are a useful little fellow and that you will take care of the house. And the Big-Blow Wind will never blow *this* house down."

And that seemed true, for the house was built of this-stone and that-stone and stuck together with safety spells.

The Bun Wife helped the Cherry Cobbler to carry his things into his new home, and that did not take very long for he does not own much. She set up his cupboard of five shelves, and on the third shelf the Cherry Cobbler found a small jar of cherry jam which he gave to the Bun Wife, for cherry jam is lovely spread on buns.

For some time after that the Cherry Cobbler was very busy indeed. Quite a number of cherry trees had been blown about by the Big-Blow Wind and were badly in need of mending, and quite a lot of cherries had to have a little brush with cherry-glow to brighten them up.

But when he had finished work he would sit on his little wooden stool and eat the porridge he had made in his porridge pan and say to himself, "What a lucky fellow I am! This is much cosier than my wooden house was. The Bun Wife still passes every day, and who knows? I may be luckier still and find the Treasure Number Six—it may be something worth having."

So the Cherry Cobbler began to search for Treasure Number Six. He dug his garden, both path and plot. Then he peered among the boughs of the elder tree that grew near his new little house, but he did not find anything. Then he became so busy mending cherries that he had little time for searching.

But one day when he took his bright little shoes from their corner, he found a sunbeam tangled in the buckle of one of them.

"Ha, what is this?" cried the Cherry Cobbler. "My little stone house only needs a sunbeam lantern to make it the nicest house in the world!" And with great care he freed the sunbeam from his buckle and set it in a lantern the Treasure Witch had left behind.

And there it twinkled and danced for a moment or two, trying to find a way out.

"Do not worry, my pretty sunbeam," said the Cherry Cobbler. "You will be quite safe in my lantern, and I will set you on a high place on my wall where no one can hurt you."

But the sunbeam only cried, "Let me out, let me out! I cannot live in this horrid little box where my wings have no room to move!"

"You have no wings," said the Cherry Cobbler.

But the sunbeam cried, "I *have* wings! You cannot see them because they are magic wings."

"Then you must draw them close to you," said the Cherry Cobbler, "just as I draw mine. Then you will have plenty of room."

"But I shall die for lack of food anyway," cried the sunbeam. "Already I am growing weak, as you can see."

"You are quite bright enough for my new little house," said the Cherry Cobbler, for he did not mean to lose sunbeam. "And I will halve my porridge, and at teatime you shall have half my bun."

But the sunbeam cried in a sad little voice, "I don't like porridge, and I *hate* buns! Only the sun can give me the food I need. Let me out, let me out or I shall die!"

Then the Cherry Cobbler was sad too, for he saw that his bright little sunbeam was less bright, and that he must let it go. And he remembered how the Bun Wife had been a friend to him when he was having a bad time, and how the Treasure Witch had let him have her little stone house when his wooden one had been blown to the ground and had asked for only a small jar of cherry jam as rent. So he felt it was maybe *his* turn to be kind.

He took the lantern to the open door of his new little house and said in a sad little voice, "Go then, little sunbeam, since you must."

And in a flash the sunbeam spread its magic wings and flew away.

And really, it was about time, for most of the other sunbeams had already gone home.

As for the Cherry Cobbler, he thought he would sit on his little wooden stool and shed a few tears, but he had only just closed his door when he heard a knock and had to open it again. There was the Big Cherry Farmer—and in such a state!

The Big Cherry Farmer cried, "Oh, dear Cherry Cobbler, do come this very minute and find out what is the matter with my cherries! They are all so cross and fussy, I am afraid they will be too sour to eat."

"Ah, I know what is the matter with *them*," said the Cherry Cobbler, while he looked for his medicine bag. "They haven't had enough sun. I can't do anything about that but I *can* give them a tiny spot of quietness, and when they have had a good night's rest they will be quite cheerful and ready for a sunny day."

"*If* we have a sunny day!" cried the Big Cherry Farmer. "I am told that a lot of greedy people try to bottle sunbeams or hoard them so that they get more than their share."

The Cherry Cobbler turned as red as a cherry but he said in a firm tone, "Oh, I think that is not done any more! And there will be lots of sun for everybody."

When they reached the cherry farm, he flew here and there among the cherries and gave to each one a

spot of quietness. He was so quick that the Big Cherry Farmer could not watch him, and he soon went away to do a job of his own, knowing that all would be well.

And indeed the cherries soon quietened and fell asleep.

When the Cherry Cobbler reached home he was very tired and thought he would go to bed early. So when someone tapped at his door he was not pleased. He called out in a tired way, "I am going to bed. Please come back in the morning."

And a sweet voice said, "I am the Tawny Owl that lives in the tree behind your elder tree. Can you come soon and help me push a stone out of my nest? It is bound by a spell and will not move."

The Cherry Cobbler at once opened the door. "Is it a cherry stone?" he asked. "For the only spells I know are cherry spells."

"Alas, it is not a cherry stone," said the Tawny Owl sadly.

"Well, never mind," said the Cherry Cobbler. "Tonight I am too tired to move anything, but tomorrow I will come along and see what I can do."

"Thank you, neighbour," said the Tawny Owl, and went away.

The next day was sunny, and when the Cherry Cobbler went to look at the Big Cherry Farmer's cherries he had dosed, they were as bright and happy as you please, and it was easy to see that there would not be a sour cherry among them.

The Big Cherry Farmer said, "You have made a good job of them, and I will give you six jars of cherry jam instead of three. My wife will send one of the boys along with them."

Hearing this good news, the Cherry Cobbler hurried home happily to his little stone house; and since he had some time to spare he thought he would dig over his flowerbed again, for he *might* have missed Treasure Number Six. He was just turning over a spadeful of earth when a bright sunbeam came dancing by.

"Let me tell you this," said the sunbeam. "You will not find Treasure Number Six in your garden, for

there is nothing there! I know, for I have danced over every little bit of it. I am telling you this because you were kind and let me out of that horrid dark box. One good turn deserves another."

"Since you know so much," said the Cherry Cobbler, "why not tell me where the Treasure is hidden?"

"I cannot, because I do not know," said the sunbeam. "All I can tell you is that it is hidden in a place where you have never looked, and within three dancing steps of the elder tree." And with that it danced away.

The Cherry Cobbler at once put away his spade, for he had no wish to dig for something that was not there. And because the sunbeam had spoken of the Elder Tree the Cherry Cobbler remembered he had told the Tawny Owl he would come along and try to help him to move a stone from his nest. So as soon as the six jars of cherry jam had been brought by the farmer's boy, the Cherry Cobbler put one or two useful things into his medicine bag and hurried to the tree just behind the elder tree.

The Tawny Owl was looking out for him. "You have come at a good time," he said, "for I am the only one at home. If you look from the other side you can see the stone."

The Cherry Cobbler peered into the nest. "Goodness me, it is a glow-worm!" he cried.

"I think it looks like a beetle," said the Tawny Owl, "but it is really a pebble. It is made of stone, and if you had had to sleep for a week with that in your nest you would know about it!"

"But how did it get there?" asked the Cherry Cobbler. "It is made of stone and cannot fly."

"The Treasure Witch asked if she might hide it there since it is one of her best treasures," said the Tawny Owl. "She said she would take it with her

when she went; but she went away nearly a month ago and it is still there. All the packing she put round it has worn away and it is harder than ever!"

"Why, it must be Treasure Number Six that the Treasure Witch could not remember about!" cried the Cherry Cobbler. "She has looked everywhere for it."

"She did not look in my nest!" said the Tawny Owl in rather a cross tone. "And that is where she put it!"

"Well, anyhow, it is quite small. I can easily get it out," cried the Cherry Cobbler, and he flew into the nest and gave a hard tug at the pebble.

But it did not move.

"There, you see!" cried the Tawny Owl. "I told you it was held by a spell. There are some words and figures written on the stone, which I have learnt by heart. But I can't make out what they mean."

And he said very slowly and clearly and close to the Cherry Cobbler's ear:

"Add One and Two and Three
and my Number you will see."

"Ah, that is easy!" cried the Cherry Cobbler and he brought from his bag a piece of slate and, sitting on the rim of the nest, he wrote on it these figures and drew a line under them.

And when he had added them up he laughed and called to the Tawny Owl: "The answer is *six!*"

"Ah, I never thought of that," said the Tawny Owl. "I cannot add up figures, only eggs."

"Let us shout 'Come along, Number Six!'" said the Cherry Cobbler. "And at the same time pull or peck."

So both of them got into the nest and the Tawny Owl got ready to peck and the Cherry Cobbler to pull. Both of them shouted "Come along, Number Six!"

And they pecked or pulled with all their might. They need not have pecked or pulled half as hard, for the Treasure came away quite easily and the Cherry Cobbler wrapped it in a soft cherry duster and put it in his medicine bag.

"On Friday I am visiting the Treasure Witch to pay my rent," said the Cherry Cobbler, "and I will take the Treasure with me." With that he picked up his medicine bag, said goodbye and went off home.

On Friday the Cherry Cobbler put a small jar of cherry jam in his pocket and picked up his medicine bag and set off for the new house of the Treasure Witch, which he knew to be far, far away from Cherry Common. He was as tired as could be when he got there, but the Treasure Witch knew he would come to pay his rent, so he found her at home.

When she caught sight of the Cherry Cobbler, she cried, "I can see a small jar of cherry jam sticking out of your pocket, and surely that was heavy enough for you to carry! Why bring your medicine bag, my little Cherry Cobbler? It's true, I have three cherry trees in my new garden, but each one is as healthy as can be!"

"Ah, I may take a look at them later," said the Cherry Cobbler, quite forgetting how tired he was. "Wait till you see what I have in my bag!" And he took from the medicine bag Treasure Number Six and unwrapped it from the cherry duster.

The Treasure Witch was so delighted and surprised

that she danced a little dance. The dishes on her shelves danced, too, and, to the surprise of the

Cherry Cobbler, the little stone glow-worm danced also, shedding a little green light like a tiny moonbeam as it moved.

When she had had enough of dancing, the Treasure Witch remembered the Cherry Cobbler and cried: "It is indeed Treasure Number Six, and the most useful one of all. It gives me just enough light when I am working on my most secret spells, and I haven't been able to do any of them since I lost the Treasure. Where did you find it, my little friend?"

"In the nest of the Tawny Owl," said the Cherry

Cobbler, and he told the Treasure Witch all about how he found her lost Treasure.

"I must send a little present to the Tawny Owl," said the Treasure Witch. "A little jar of Special Treat will please him and his family, I think. As for you, Cherry Cobbler, I shall take no more rent from you for the little stone house; it is yours from this very day."

When the Cherry Cobbler heard this wonderful news he almost wept for joy. And he cried, "Thank you twenty times, dear Treasure Witch! When I have had a look at your cherry trees, I will go back to the little house which is now my own."

The Cherry Cobbler gave only one glance at the three cherry trees, for they too seemed to be bubbling over with joy. Then he said goodbye to the Treasure Witch and offered to carry the little jar of Special Treat to the Tawny Owl. "It is not much heavier than Treasure Number Six," he said.

The Cherry Cobbler reached his little stone house in less than half the time he had taken on the going-out journey, for being happy shortens every long trip.

He sat on his little wooden stool and ate his supper

porridge and looked about his kitchen and thought, "This little house is *my very own!*"

As for the Tawny Owl, he and his family said the Special Treat was the best they had ever tasted. The Tawny Owl did not say what was in it, for the Tawny Owl never tells.

The Rabbits' Party

The Invitation

First the little left leg squeezed into the tight orange trousers, then the right one as Ragbud, the elf, dressed himself with great care. He was invited to the Rabbits' party!

Pulling his green cap neatly over his ears he stepped in front of the looking glass. Ragbud sighed a little as he looked at himself. His suit was rather old because his mummy was too poor to buy new clothes very often, but it was very clean and well pressed. She had told him to remember to give his boots an extra polish and he would look quite smart.

Everyone knows that the Rabbits' party is very grand indeed. The tunnels in the Warren where the rabbits live make wonderful places to play exciting games. Though the rabbits don't like to eat rich food themselves, they make sure their guests have lots of cream cakes, jellies and other good things.

Only those with invitations are allows to go, and Ragbud was very happy to have had one.

He called "Goodbye" to his Mummy as he ran out of the door and down the garden path.

Suddenly he noticed his boots. Oh dear! He had forgotten to polish them after all.

"Perhaps no one will notice," Ragbud thought, and he hurried on over the fields.

Soon Ragbud saw someone dressed in brightly coloured clothes coming down the hill towards him. It was a gnome. He looked as if he was on his way to the party too, for he carried his large, white invitation card tucked under one arm and a big paper bag under the other. The gnome wore a beautiful suit of bright blue with a shining silver belt around his fat tummy. He made Ragbud feel quite shabby.

"Hello," he cried, "are you going to the Rabbits' party?"

The gnome stopped and said in a very superior voice, "Of course. Can't you see my invitation card? And who might you be?" he asked rudely.

Ragbud was rather surprised but he said, "I'm

Ragbud, the elf, and I'm going to the Warren too. What's your name?"

The gnome looked more superior than ever. "I am Trampin the gnome," he answered, "the most splendid gnome in the district. Look at my new suit. I shall look smarter than anybody else at the party. But what is this nonsense about *you* going? They certainly won't let you in wearing that dingy orange suit. You say your name is Ragbud. It ought to be Rags from the look of you," and the unkind gnome roared with laughter, jumping up and down.

Opening his huge paper bag, Trampin then took out a large cream bun and began to eat it greedily.

"I know I'm not very smart," said Ragbud sadly, "but my suit is clean and nicely pressed. Besides, my mummy patched it very neatly."

"Patched it!" said Trampin, laughing even more. "Fancy having patches on your suit!"

He walked off into the woods. Ragbud followed close behind him while the gnome chattered over his shoulder all the way to the Rabbits' Warren. Trampin boasted and boasted on and on about how fine he would look at the Rabbits' party. Poor Ragbud became sadder and sadder.

Then they passed a big notice which said, "Witches' Leap" in large white letters. Near it was a

wide hole in the ground where the earth had fallen away. One side was higher than the other and the lower side was covered with soft, loose sand.

"I can jump that easily any time I feel like it," said Trampin proudly, "but not while I'm wearing my fine new suit."

It looked an awfully wide jump to Ragbud, and he didn't think he would like even to try it.

At the Warren

At last they reached the Warren. Standing outside, bending over a table, was an old grey rabbit. On the table lay the invitation cards he had taken from other guests.

The rude gnome marched straight up to the table shouting, "Here I am, Trampin the gnome. Let me pass, so that I can show everyone my lovely clothes."

The old rabbit did not look up. "Your invitation card, please," he said quite politely, and he put out his hand towards Ragbud.

Ragbud thought the rabbit had made a mistake. Trampin was staring angrily at him. Then slowly Ragbud held out his card.

"Yes," said the rabbit, "that looks all right, Ragbud the elf." He turned round at last and looked down at him. "Quite smart." Then he noticed Ragbud's dirty boots.

"Dearie me," he said, "that won't do at all. You can't go in like that."

Poor Ragbud went red. "I know they are rather dirty," he said, "but you see, I was in such a hurry to get here that I quite forgot to clean them."

The grey rabbit looked at him kindly and said, "Never mind, if you run home quickly and polish your boots you will still be back in time for the cakes and jellies."

The gnome was still holding out his card.

"Ah, yes," said the rabbit, without looking up. "You are Trampin the gnome, I believe." Then for the first time he looked at the rude guest. As he caught sight of the splendid blue suit he put one hand up to cover his eyes and stepped back with a gasp. "My goodness!" he cried. "We rabbits are not used to anything as bright as that. Why, we have had to put lights in our dark tunnels specially for the guests as it is. You must go home and change."

Trampin asked crossly, "Don't you like my fine new blue suit?"

"I like it," said the grey rabbit, "but it is too bright for us, that is all."

"But I can't go home," said Trampin, feeling rather sorry for himself. "I live miles away over the hills."

"Then," said the rabbit, "you had better go back to Witches' Leap. Jump over that twenty times to take some of the brightness out of your suit. It will get rid of a lot of fat, too. You would never get down our rabbit hole anyway; you have eaten far too many cream buns. You will miss the nice tea, but you will still be in time for the games."

Trampin looked at the hole. It was true. He could

never get down such a small hole as long as he was so fat. Making a face at Ragbud, Trampin hurried off. Ragbud ran home as fast as he could go.

Tramp and Rags

Ragbud arrived home in a few minutes and told his mummy what had happened. He took his polishing brushes and cleaned his boots till they shone. Then off he ran again, but when he got to the gate he suddenly remembered Trampin jumping twenty times over the Witches' Leap.

"My goodness," thought the elf, "by the time he

has finished jumping into the sand his boots will be dirtier than mine were, and then the rabbit will stop him again. I had better take him my brushes."

So he turned back to get them, then ran quickly to Witches' Leap.

Trampin was busy jumping and was thinner already. His suit was now covered with sand.

Ragbud saw the big bag of cream cakes lying by

the path. "I do wish they were mine," he thought. He left the brushes beside the bag for Trampin to find and ran off once more.

Suddenly he stopped again. "Trampin will almost certainly tear his suit and will have nothing to patch it with," he said to himself. "I must take him home so that Mummy can patch him up. It means I shall miss tea too but I don't want Trampin to miss all of the party."

So back he went again and reached Witches' Leap just as the gnome had finished jumping.

Trampin had gone back for his cakes, seen Ragbud's brushes and had pounced on them. He was busily cleaning his boots as Ragbud came up to him.

"Ha, you, is it?" said Trampin. "You dropped your brushes and now I'm using them. You have missed tea as well, having to come back for them," and he laughed rudely.

"I left them there for you," said Ragbud. "Now I have come back to see if you have torn your suit."

Yes, there was a large tear in the seat of the gnome's trousers. Trampin nearly cried, but Ragbud told him his mummy would mend the tear.

"All right," grumbled Trampin, "that rabbit won't let me in like this."

So off they went back to Ragbud's home.

His mummy was very helpful. She got out her sewing box, found a piece of bright blue cloth and quickly patched the tear.

Trampin took out his last cream bun and ate it greedily. "I like cream buns," he said. "I suppose Ragbud ate all his before coming out, or he would have some too."

"Oh dear no!" said Ragbud's mummy. "Ragbud never has cream buns."

The gnome could not believe it. "But he *must* have had cream buns," he cried, "or he would have taken mine when he put the polishing brushes down."

"Good gracious no!" said Ragbud's mummy. "Ragbud would not have taken your buns even if he had been starving."

Trampin was so surprised by this that he quite forgot to thank her as he set off once more with Ragbud. "I am hungry now after all that jumping," grumbled Trampin. "What a pity we have missed tea!"

"Never mind," said Ragbud, "we'll have some fun at the party and then you must come home with me for supper."

"Do you really mean that?" asked Trampin.

"Yes," said Ragbud, "I like helping you."

The gnome, no longer so fat or so superior, took Ragbud's arm. "You are a funny little chap," he said. "You brought me brushes to clean my boots. You didn't take my buns when you must have been longing for them. Then you missed your tea by taking me home to have my trousers patched and now you are asking me to supper. After all the horrible things I said about *your* patched clothes, I feel ashamed."

"But they were quite true," said Ragbud kindly. "My suit is worn and patched." Then he smiled and said, "But now you are patched too. Your name should be Tramp because you look like one!"

Trampin went very red and began to look cross. Then suddenly he began to laugh loudly.

"You are quite right," he cried. So off they ran together, hand in hand.

Back at the Warren, the grey rabbit was still bent over his table.

Up rushed Trampin. "Here I am, Tramp the gnome," he shouted.

Then it was Ragbud's turn. "Here I am, Rags the elf," he called out.

The old rabbit peered at them over his spectacles. "Off you go," he said. "You are lucky. King Rabbit

made such a long speech that tea hasn't started yet, so you will still be in time for your cakes and jellies."

"Hurrah!" cried the two new friends together, as they dived into the rabbit hole. Trampin pushed

Ragbud in first and then slipped in behind quite easily because he was so much thinner.

The old grey rabbit gazed after them, and then he raised one eyebrow in surprise. For the last thing he saw was a neat blue patch on Trampin's trousers as he wriggled down the rabbit hole.

Jack-a-Dandy

How Jack-a-Dandy got his Name

Jack-a-Dandy lived long, long ago, all alone in a funny little house.

This house had white walls, a red roof and a little green door. It stood at the far end of town. People said it was so small there was no room for anyone else when Jack went in! But then he was a very fat little man.

There was an odd thing about Jack's house. Each room was filled with boxes.

There were so many boxes there was no room in the house for more than one table, one chair and a small footstool. So Jack had to make his bed on the top of a big box.

Every box was full to the brim with fine things to wear. There were rich coats and cloaks of silk and satin, hats with feathers in them, and dozens of fine leather shoes. All these things were of as many colours as the rainbow—pink, blue, purple, green, yellow. No one in all that land had so many fine, rich clothes to wear as Jack-a-Dandy.

He had a fresh coat, cloak and hat for every day in the year. As for his shoes, no one could count how many pairs he had.

He was so fond of all the fine clothes in those boxes! And how he loved to try on each in turn and admire himself in his mirror!

He used to put on a different coat three times a day. First he would wear a green one, then a red, then a blue. Now and then he even wore two coats at once!

Every afternoon he would dress himself carefully

in a rich coat and cloak of silk and a hat with gold lace all over it. Then he would take a walk round the town, just to show himself off.

He was so proud of himself and of the fine things he wore that he would not mix with the people of the town. He used to strut past them on his fat little legs with his nose in the air! And he never greeted his neighbours.

"I am far too grand to mix with such poor people," he would mutter to himself.

But, of course, people did not like such silly, proud ways. "He is just a stuck-up little dandy," they said.

A dandy is someone who is very smart and very proud of what he wears.

And that was how this funny little man got the name of Jack-a-Dandy.

Plum Cake and Sugar Candy

Now there was something else that Jack-a-Dandy loved as well as fine clothes. That something else was sweet things to eat. He was just as fond of cakes and sweets as any boy or girl.

He liked every kind of cake and every kind of sweet no matter what it was. But the kind of cake he liked best of all was *plum cake*. And there was no sweet he liked as much as *sugar candy*.

But there was one thing that made Jack very sad. In the town where he lived, there was no plum cake or sugar candy to be had. There was no shop that sold even a tiny bit of plum cake or a single stick of candy.

Of course, the boys and girls of the town found this very hard when they had some money to spend. Still, sometimes they were lucky enough to have cake and candy made for them at home. But Jack did not know how to make such things, so it was not often that he was able to have the treat he liked best.

One day Jack set off from his house for a walk. The road he took ran by a little wood. Very soon, among the trees, he saw a tiny white house.

"Who can live there?" Jack said to himself. "I have never seen that house before."

He went up to the door. There was a big green board with these words on it:

PLUM CAKE

AND

SUGAR CANDY

SOLD HERE

Jack jumped with excitement. Then he took a peep in at the window. It was set out like the window of a shop. And it was full of piles and piles of plum cake and rows and rows of sugar candy!

Jack rushed into the funny little shop, where he found an ugly old lady in a red cloak.

"What can I get for you, sir?" she asked.

"I want six pounds of plum cake and ten sticks of sugar candy!" said Jack.

The old lady put the cake and the candy into a big bag and Jack paid for them. Then he set off for home again as fast as he could go.

"How glad I am," said he to himself, "that at last I have found a cake-and-candy shop so near home! Now I can have these nice things as often as I like!"

What a feast Jack had that night! He had never had any cake or candy in all his life that was half so good as this.

Soon he began to go two or three times a week to the little shop in the wood. The old lady came to know him very well and took care to save all her cake and candy for him.

The boys and girls of the town found the shop too, but there was never any cake or candy for them. Jack-a-Dandy bought every bit of it! They said this was not fair. But Jack did not stop to think of anyone else when plum cake and sugar candy were to be had.

He grew to love cake and candy more and more every day. He was soon so fond of these sweet things that the boys and girls made up a little song about him.

This was the way they used to tease him. When he took a walk round the town, they would join hands and dance behind him in a row singing;

"Handy, pandy, Jack-a-Dandy
Loves plum cake and sugar candy."

How he Spoilt his New Coat

One day Jack-a-Dandy put on some grand new clothes that he had never worn before. The coat and hat were of blue satin and gold lace and the coat was trimmed with fine white fur.

Jack was going out for the day to visit a great lord whom he knew, so he had made up his mind to be very, very smart.

He went down the street with his nose high in the air. How funny he looked, with his little fat body in those bright clothes and his little short legs!

The boys and girls left their play to watch him go by. At last they joined hands, and came after him with a hop, skip, and a jump; and then they sang:

"Handy, pandy, Jack-a-Dandy
Loves plum cake and sugar candy."

But Jack's mind was so full of his fine dress, and of what a splendid sight he was, that he did not care a bit. He would not even look at them.

After a while he left the town and came to a road that led to the lord's castle. On one side of this road there was a big pond full of muddy water.

Jack did not look at the pond as he went by. But all at once he heard someone call out, "Help! help! or I shall sink!"

Jack ran up at once. There, in the middle of the pond, was an old woman, up to her neck in water.

"Help! help! or I shall sink!" she cried again as Jack came near.

For once Jack did not stop to think about clothes. With a jump and a splash, he was in the pond too. Oh, how cold and dirty that horrid water was! But he took hold of the old lady, and was soon able to drag her to the bank.

At last they were both on dry land again. The old woman shook with fear and cold, for her cloak was soaking and covered in mud.

As for Jack-a-Dandy, he was not at all smart now! The lovely satin coat was wet from neck to hem and over it there were marks of nasty green slime and dark brown mud. It would never be the same again. His fine new coat was spoilt for ever.

The Wish

"Oh, dear! What a mess I am in!" cried poor Jack. Then he looked at the old woman. To his surprise, Jack saw that it was the old woman who sold plum cake and sugar candy at the little shop in the wood!

"Dear me," she said. "I am so sorry, this is all my fault. What can I do to make up to you for the loss of your fine new coat?"

"I must go home at once," said Jack. "I shall not be

able to go to my lord's grand castle in this state. Goodbye, lady."

"Wait," said the old woman, "I must do something for you, as you have done so much for me."

She thought for a second and then cried, "I know what I will do! I will give you a wish!"

"A wish!" cried Jack.

"Yes. Some people call me a witch," went on the old woman, "but I never harm anybody, and to those who do me a good turn, I can give a wish that will come true. Now, what is there that you wish for? Tell me and you shall have it, whatever it may be."

It took Jack a long time to think this over. What should he wish for? More fine things to wear? A grand new house and a great deal of money? He was just about to speak, when the old woman began to sing in a soft voice;

"Handy, pandy, Jack-a-Dandy
Loves plum cake and sugar candy."

"Plum cake and sugar candy for ever and ever! I will not have anything else to eat as long as I live! Oh! I am sure I shall never get tired of them!"

"Very well," said the old woman, with a smile, "we shall see!"

Too Much of a Good Thing

When Jack got home, he found he was soaked to the skin and very, very cold.

"I will have a bowl of nice, hot bread and milk," he said, "and then I will go to bed."

He soon got the bread and milk ready. But, when he sat down to eat it there was no bread and milk to be seen anywhere! On his plate, instead of the bowl, was a large, round plum cake and a long stick of sugar candy!

What a shock Jack got at first! Then he began to think of his wish, "Plum cake and sugar candy for ever and ever."

85

"Oh, well," he said, "I don't mind." And he ate up the cake and candy and went off to bed.

Every day after that the same thing happened. Everything he got ready to eat would change to cake and candy before his eyes.

If he went to buy meat, bread or fish, he found it was cake and candy by the time he got home.

At first he liked this very much because he was so fond of plum cake and sugar candy, it did not seem, at first, as if he could ever have too much of them.

But finally, he began to get rather tired of plum cake and sugar candy for breakfast! Plum cake and sugar candy for dinner! Plum cake and sugar candy for supper! The sight of other nice food made him sad, because when he tried to taste it, it would turn to plum cake and sugar candy.

At last he began to feel sick at the sight of cake and candy. Then he grew to hate the taste of them.

He never went near the little shop in the wood now. He had no need and no wish to do so. And oh! how cross he grew when the boys and girls danced at his heels and sang:

> *"Handy, pandy, Jack-a-Dandy*
> *Loves plum cake and sugar candy."*

"Oh, now I know that one can have too much of a good thing!" said Jack.

"Just for a Change"

At last, Jack made up his mind to go and see the old woman at the little shop in the wood.

"I will ask her to take back the wish she gave me," said he. "I am so tired of plum cake and sugar candy! I don't think I ever want to taste them again!"

The very sight of the old woman's shop window made him feel quite ill. He found her in the shop and told her his tale.

"Oh, please, *please* take back the wish!" he said at last.

But the old woman only smiled.

"I cannot take your wish back," she said, "but, if you like, I can change it for you a little. Now, Jack-a-Dandy, I know you love fine things to wear as much as you once loved cake and candy. You love to put on a fine coat every day, don't you? Well, just for a change, every day that you wear a coat that is old or dirty or torn, you are to eat whatever you wish. But, on the days that you choose to wear a fine coat, you will have only cake and candy to eat. And this is all I can do for you."

Jack in a Fix

When Jack got home he went to one of his boxes and took out a dirty, ragged old coat. At any other time, the sight of such a poor thing to wear would have made Jack turn up his nose.

But he quickly pulled it on and sat down to a big plate of bread and butter, and ate it all!

So, for some time, Jack wore the oldest and shabbiest coats he could find. He had everything to

eat he could wish for, but he would not touch one thing that was sweet. He did not even want even to think of plum cake or sugar candy for a long, long time.

All this time he stayed in the house and would not go out at all. He did not want the townspeople to see him in his shabby coats.

But one fine day, he grew tired of all this and did not stop to think of the old witch's words. He put on a rich red silk coat and a cloak of green satin. Then he set off to walk round the town with his nose in the air, just as he used to do.

But, oh dear! When he got home he found only plum cake and sugar candy to eat for the rest of the day! How he hated them! He would not touch his supper at all that night.

Jack *was* in a fix. He loved fine things to wear, but whenever he wore them, he could have only plum cake and sugar candy to eat. At the same time, if he wished to eat anything else, he had to wear dirty old coats that were all in rags. And he hated to wear such shabby clothes, as much as he now hated to eat plum cake and sugar candy, because he was such a dandy!

"New Coats for Old"

At last, one day, a strange old man came to the town where Jack lived. He wore a long coat that was half black and half yellow, and on his back was a heavy pack. He had a great white beard that came down to his knees and his eyes were bright blue and very merry.

Down the street he went, and on his way he cried out, "New coats for old! New coats for old! Bring out your old coats and you shall have new ones!"

A crowd came round him and he began to open his big pack. It was full of fine new silk coats of every sort and shade. And everybody in the town happily gave up all their old coats and got new ones in their place. How smart they all were!

At last someone said, "Where is Jack-a-Dandy? Why has he not come to get his share of such fine things?"

"Jack-a-Dandy!" said the queer old man. "I will go and find him." And away he went to Jack's house, crying, "New coats for old!"

But when Jack heard him and saw the fine things in his pack, he said sadly:

"I do not want any more new coats. I shall never wear smart clothes again."

And he felt so miserable that he told the old man his sad story.

"I never mean to taste plum cake or sugar candy again as long as I live," he said. "So that means I must wear shabby coats for the rest of my life. But, oh dear! How sorry I am!"

"You have been very silly and vain and greedy," said the old man, "to think so much of fine things to wear and sweet things to eat. That old witch at the shop in the wood has been able to play a fine trick on you. But I think I can help you."

An Odd Coat

With these words, the old man took from his pack the oddest coat Jack had ever seen.

One half of it was of rich pink satin and silver cloth and lace and the other half was just a mass of dirty old rags! Jack could only stand and stare at it. But the old man held it up with a laugh.

"I will give you this to wear," said he. "You see, it is new as well as old, and smart as well as shabby. So it is bound to be just the right thing for you! And, every day you put it on, you may eat whatever you please."

"But must I wear it always?" cried Jack, for he began to think that such a coat was far worse than

one that was all rags. How the people of the town would laugh at him when they saw it!

"You must wear this coat and no other for a year and a day," said the old man. "And all that time, you must go among the good folk of this town. But you must not be either proud or vain. You are no better and no worse than they, you know. One half of you will be a dandy, but the other half will be just a ragged Jack. If you do this for a year and a day, you will be able to wear what you like and eat what you wish after that. I think you will even be able to like plum cake and sugar candy once again."

Happy at Last

When the old man had gone, leaving the odd coat behind him, Jack made up his mind he would wear it. He *did* so wish to become like other people once more!

So he put on the coat and went out in the town. But this time he did not strut about with his nose in the air. He was not quite a dandy, for half of him was in rags, so he had no cause to be proud.

The townspeople stood still to stare at him and at

first they began to laugh. But Jack tried not to mind their smiles. He had made up his mind to do as the old man had told him. So he stopped to speak with one or two people, and did his best to be kind and cheerful.

At last he told them all his story and how silly and greedy he had been. "But I mean to change now," he said.

And he kept his word. Every day after that he went out in the town in that odd coat. He did not show any pride now and soon he did not think of his looks at all. His mind was full of other things and of how he could make other people happy.

So everyone grew to love him and, when the year and the day had gone by, Jack made a grand dinner for all the town.

Jack wore a nice new coat, but he was not a bit proud of it. He was glad to put away his rags, but he had put away his pride as well, you see.

At the dinner, an odd thing took place. On the table, for the sake of the boys and girls, were plum cake and sugar candy. To please them all, Jack took a small taste himself, and he found that the cake and candy were nicer than ever before!

But, this time, he would not eat too much of them. "Enough is as good as a feast!" said Jack-a-Dandy.

The Little Red Cow

Once upon a time there lived a man and his wife who had two little girls.

The elder girl was ugly and very bad-tempered, while the younger one was so pretty and sweet that everyone loved her, except her father, her mother and her sister.

They were jealous of her lovely face and gentle ways, so they made her do all the hard work in the house, and she had to work in the fields as well. They never gave her nice food—all she had was porridge and sometimes a little sour milk. She never wore anything but old and shabby clothes, though her sister had many fine dresses made of silk and satin.

Part of the girl's work was to look after the cattle in the fields. Among her father's cattle there was a little red cow.

One day this little cow saw the girl crying bitterly over her bowl of sour milk, and it said, "Give that sour milk to the dog and come along with me."

So the poor girl followed the red cow across the fields, and after a while they came to a little wood.

In the middle of the wood stood a tiny white house. They went in, and there on the table was a good dinner, all ready to be eaten. It was the finest feast the girl had ever seen. There were roasted chicken and hams, and cakes, jellies, cream and many other good things.

The little red cow and the girl sat down and ate as much as they wanted. When they had finished, they went back to the fields to look after the animals.

The next day the same thing happened and every day after it was the same. The little girl ate a good dinner in the tiny white house, and every day she grew more and more pretty.

Her father and mother and sister were very angry when they saw this. They had hoped all the work they made her do would soon take away her beauty.

They began to watch her, and one day they saw her go with the little red cow to the house where the feast was spread.

Then they were angrier than ever. They said the little red cow must be killed and told the girl that she herself must chop off its head with an axe.

When the little girl heard this she began to cry, for she dearly loved the little red cow. But it came to her and said, "Do not cry any more. When they are waiting for you to chop off my head, you must jump on my back instead, and I will run away with you."

So the girl dried her eyes. And a little later her parents gave her the axe and brought the little red cow out of its stall for her to kill.

But, instead of chopping off the little cow's head, she threw the axe away very quickly, and jumped on to its back.

Then they set off and ran away so fast that nobody was able to catch them.

On they went for many miles until they came to a river where rushes grew.

As the poor girl's clothes were nearly all in rags, she gathered the rushes and made them into a coat for herself.

Then they set off again, and the little red cow ran on and on until they came to a King's palace.

There the little girl asked if the King wanted a servant and was told that a kitchen maid was needed in the palace, and that, if she wished, she might stay.

And the girl said, "I will stay, if you will let the little red cow stay with me."

So the little red cow also stayed at the palace, and because the little girl always wore her coat of rushes, the other servants gave her the name Rushie-coat. But they treated her kindly, and she worked so well and so hard that everyone was pleased with her.

Christmas came, and on Christmas Day the King and his guests and all his servants went to church. All except Rushie-coat, who stayed at the palace to cook the dinner.

After they had all gone, the little red cow came to

her, and said, "Would you like to go to church with the rest?"

"I should like it more than anything else," said Rushie-coat; "but as you see, I have no proper clothes to wear. I have only my coat of rushes; and then I must cook the dinner in time for the King's return. I cannot leave that."

"Oh, that is nothing!" said the little red cow. "You may leave the dinner to me, and I will give you some new clothes to wear."

So the little red cow went out, and a little later came back with a beautiful dress of gold and silver and a pair of golden shoes."

Rushie-coat dressed herself in her fine new clothes, put on the golden shoes, combed out her long golden hair and set out for the church.

But, before she left the kitchen, she went to the great kitchen fire, and said;

"Each coal make another burn,
And each spit make another turn,
And each pot make another play,
Till I come home from church on Christmas Day."

Then she went to church and sat amongst the King's guests. Everyone wondered who the beautiful lady in the gold-and-silver dress could be. They thought she must be some strange princess whom they had never seen or heard of before.

But nobody guessed that it was Rushie-coat, the King's kitchen maid.

When the King saw her he at once fell in love with her, but not because of her fine dress. He looked only at her lovely face and thought how sweet and gentle she seemed. He made up his mind to try to find out who she was.

But Rushie-coat left before the rest, so that she might get home in time to take off her dress and finish cooking the dinner.

When the King saw she was going, he started up to follow her. But as she rushed past him out of the door, in her hurry, she left one of her little golden shoes behind her on the step.

The King picked up the shoe and went back to his place.

"It is no bigger than a fairy's," he said to himself.

Rushie-coat got home in safety, and soon after, the King and his guests and servants returned to the palace.

Everyone praised the dinner and said it was the best they had ever tasted.

But the King could not forget the beautiful lady who had been at the church.

Next day he sent a servant through all his kingdom with the golden shoe. Each lady in the land was to try it on.

The King promised that the lady whom the golden shoe fitted exactly should marry him, and he would make her his queen.

The servant went all over the kingdom, but there was not one lady whose foot the shoe would fit, because it was so small.

At last he came to the house of Rushie-coat's father. Now, Rushie-coat's elder sister had little feet too, and, of course, she tried on the golden shoe, because she wanted to marry the King.

It almost fitted her, but not quite. So, when the servant was looking another way, she clipped a little piece off each heel. Then she pushed her foot into the shoe and the servant saw that it fitted.

So he took her to the King, and said, "Sir, I have brought you the lady."

The King looked at the girl, and he saw that she was not at all like the lady he had seen at the church. He was very angry. But he had to keep his word, because he had promised to marry the lady whom the golden shoe fitted.

The wedding day came and the King rode to church on a big white horse with his bride on the saddle before him.

But, as they went along, the little red cow looked over a hedge at them and said,

> *"Clipped toes and chopped heels*
> *are on the saddle set.*
> *But pretty feet and little feet*
> *sit in the kitchen yet."*

"What is that you say?" said the King, stopping his horse.

"Oh," said his bride, "why do bother what a silly red cow says? We shall be late for church."

But the King insisted that the red cow should repeat what it had said.

So the little red cow said again:

> *"Clipped toes and chopped heels*
> *are on the saddle set.*
> *But pretty feet and little feet*
> *sit in the kitchen yet."*

The King turned his horse and rode back to the palace. He went straight to the kitchen and found Rushie-coat sitting by the fireside shelling peas. The King recognized her at once because she was so pretty, in spite of her coat of rushes.

She slipped on the golden shoe, and it fitted her exactly.

Then the King kissed her, and laughed and said, "I was sure I had got the wrong one at first!"

So Rushie-coat and the King were married that very day. And of course the little red cow was at the wedding.

The King and Queen took the little red cow to live with them always. They built a house for it and treated it well, because it had always been so kind to Rushie-coat, the poor kitchen maid.

The Magic Duck

Once upon a time there lived, in a far-off land in the north, a boy whose name was Ivan.

Ivan's father and mother, who were very poor, had their home in a little hut in a forest, not far from a big town.

Little Ivan was a handsome boy—brave and strong, with bright eyes and such a happy face that everyone was glad to see him and speak to him.

His father and mother were so poor that Ivan was often dressed in rags. But he was not at all unhappy. In the summer, it was easy for him to get work in the town and he was able to earn a little money to buy food.

In the winter food was very scarce and Ivan was often hungry. Sometimes he ate only one meal a day, but he never grumbled about this hard life, for he had learned to be content with very little.

One cold evening in winter, little Ivan's father came home with a loaf of bread. It was all the food he had been able to buy that day and he cut it into three parts, one for his wife, one for little Ivan and one for himself.

Then he sat down before the stove to eat his poor supper.

Now, as he was eating, an ugly little fairy, who lived behind the stove, crept up behind him.

She snatched the poor man's piece of bread out of his hand and ate it up herself.

When the man saw that his supper was gone, he grew angry and cried to the fairy:

"Give me back my supper or I shall die of hunger!"

"I cannot give you back your supper," said the

fairy; "but I will give you instead a duck which will lay a golden egg for you every morning."

"Where shall I find that duck?" asked Ivan's father.

"When you go to the town tomorrow," said the fairy, "you will pass a pond with a duck swimming on it. You must catch the duck and carry it home. It is a magic duck and it will bring you good fortune."

The very next morning Ivan's father set off for the town. After a while he came to the pond where he found the duck swimming, just as the fairy had said. It was a fine large bird, with feathers as white as snow.

He caught it quickly and took it home to his wife. She put it in a basket, and when, at the end of an hour, she lifted it up, it had laid a big golden egg.

Little Ivan danced for joy when he saw it. "Now we shall not be poor or hungry any more," he cried.

His father took the egg to the town and sold it for a large sum of money. Then he went off to market and bought some food.

Little Ivan and his father and mother had a fine supper that night. They ate all kinds of good things, such as Ivan had never tasted before. And in the morning they found that the duck had laid another golden egg.

Day after day it was the same. Each morning the duck laid an egg of pure gold and little Ivan's father sold all the eggs it laid.

He soon had made so much money that he was able to buy a grand house and many fine things. Every year he grew richer, but he would never tell anyone the secret of his riches. Only his wife and little Ivan knew of the duck which laid a golden egg each morning.

One day, a young man, who was a servant in the house, found out the secret. Ivan's father was not at

home and, by chance, the servant discovered where the magic duck was kept and he watched little Ivan's mother lifting it out of the basket.

Later, he too lifted up the duck, and to his surprise saw that under one wing was written, in golden letters:

"The Man who eats this Duck will become a King."

He put the duck down again and said nothing, for he knew that neither the woman nor her husband could read.

But Ivan's mother knew the young man had seen the duck and the egg it had laid and she was very much afraid.

"Do not tell my husband what you have seen," she said. "I will give you a large bag of gold, if you promise to keep the secret."

But the servant was very sly. He wanted to eat the duck after reading the golden words beneath its

wing, so he said; "The duck will never lay any more eggs now that the secret is known. And, when your husband comes home, it is sure to tell him what you have done."

The woman began to cry. "Oh, no!" she wept. "How angry my husband will be when he finds out! What shall I do?"

"If you kill the duck and cook it," said the servant, "I will eat it. It is a magic bird, and by eating it I shall be able to make your husband forget both the duck and its golden eggs."

The woman believed what he said was true. As she was very much afraid of her husband's anger, she killed the duck at once, plucked and dressed it, and put it into the oven.

Then the servant made her go with him to the counting house where Ivan's father kept all his gold, so that she might give him the money she had promised him.

While they were there little Ivan came home from a day's skating on the great frozen river. He was very hungry but there was no one in the house, so he began to look for something to eat.

Ivan could smell the duck roasting in the kitchen and when he opened the oven door, he saw it was brown and crisp and ready to be eaten.

"Here is the very thing!" he cried happily. "What a wonderful feast I will have before Mother comes back!"

He took the duck out of the oven, put it on a big dish and began to eat it.

It tasted so good that he ate and ate until soon only the bones were left. Then, when he could eat no more, he ran out of the house again.

When his mother and the servant came back and found that the duck was gone, the woman was very afraid and the servant flew into a rage.

He told the woman she had cheated him, then he

left quickly, taking the bag of the money she had given him.

The next day little Ivan's father came home. "Where is the duck?" he said at once.

"I don't know," said his wife, for she did not dare to tell him the awful story.

Ivan's father began to search the house, but there was no duck to be found. His wife went after him, but she was afraid to tell him what had happened.

Little Ivan was playing out of doors in the snow, when his father called: "Ivan, where is the duck? I cannot find it anywhere."

Ivan came to his father at once and said: "Yesterday, when I came home, I was very hungry. There was no one in the house, but there was a fine duck roasting in the oven. So I pulled it out and ate it. I did not know it was the duck that laid the golden eggs."

When Ivan's father heard this, he was so angry that he told his son to leave the house for ever. He scolded his wife too, when he heard the whole story. Then he went away to his counting house and found that a lot of his money had gone. Without the duck he was soon a poor man again and had to give up his grand house and all the fine things in it. Then he and his wife were living in the little hut in the forest, just as they had done before.

They missed little Ivan very much, and Ivan's father was very sorry he had told his son to leave.

When he was sent away, little Ivan set off along the road weeping bitterly. He went on for many long miles until he was tired out. At last he met an old woman.

"Why are you crying, little boy?" she asked.

"My father has turned me out of the house," wept Ivan, "because I ate a duck which laid golden eggs."

And he told the old woman his sad story.

"You were wrong to eat the duck," said the old woman, "and you must try some day to make up to your father for all he has lost. But now I will tell you what to do. You must travel on till you come to the city of Moscow. When you reach it, go straight through the gates and take the first offer that is made to you."

So Ivan walked on for nine long days until he came to the city of Moscow. There he went straight through the city gates just as the old woman had told him.

To his surprise, a great crowd of people came out to meet him, waving their hands and shouting:

"Here is our King! Long live our noble King!"

What a crowd there was! They knelt before him, kissed his hands and then led him to a great palace.

More crowds met them on the way, and they too shouted and waved to the little boy. Ivan was so pleased to see that they wished to be kind to him, that he bowed and smiled in return. Then the people cheered even more than before.

When he came to the palace, one of the governors of the city told him the old King had died some days before. He had left no one to be king after him and so the people had made up their minds that the first

strange man or boy who came through the city gates should be their new king.

How glad they were to see such a fine strong boy as little Ivan! They were sure he would grow up to be a good king.

He was dressed in rich clothes of silk and fur and a gold crown was placed on his head. Then again the people came to him and cried:

"Long live our noble King!
Long live our noble King!"

Of course little Ivan had not forgotten his father and mother. He wanted to see them again very much, so he sent for them to come to the palace.

At first they were very shy, when they saw their son sitting on a grand throne and wearing a golden crown. But little Ivan was very kind to them and told them they would live in the palace with him to the end of their lives.

Little Ivan grew up to be a good, wise king, and all his people loved him. But he never forgot the magic duck that had laid the golden eggs!